I0728034

Ghost:
An Alien Scifi Romance

DEMELZA CARLTON

Copyright © 2020 Demelza Carlton

Lost Plot Press

All rights reserved.

ONE

Maia wasn't sure what woke her, but it sure was chilly in the break room tonight. Someone had probably switched off the heating to save power again, forgetting that the night shift nurses napped there when the patient load allowed it. Either that or the old wiring had shorted out again. She'd have to call Maintenance, to make sure they fixed it this time.

Then something touched her tummy,

brushing it lightly like a lover might. Problem was, Maia didn't have a lover right now.

"Aren't you a delightful specimen," a male voice crooned.

Her eyes flew open. No one called her a specimen and got away with it.

Definitely not Mr Tall, Dark and Purple, who was staring at her rounded midsection like it was his next meal.

Her breath caught in her throat. Either this was a very unfunny joke, she was hallucinating, or there was an honest to goodness alien standing over her with a syringe.

She squinted at the vial he'd stuck the syringe into. No way was she letting him inject her with a sedative. Stars only knew what he'd done to her before she woke up.

Good thing she'd taken those self defence classes at the hospital back home. The ones for dealing with difficult patients, or particularly violent ones. First she disabled him with a well-placed elbow, before a deft twist transferred the syringe from his hand to hers.

She didn't hesitate – she knew a dose meant for her wouldn't kill him. She stabbed the needle deep into his neck and shoved the plunger down until all the liquid was gone.

"Hey, you…" he slurred, twisting away from her before she could take the syringe out. But the sedative was already taking effect, so he slumped over her legs, a dead, drooling weight.

Maia slid out from under him, and hopped off the gurney. It was the high tech sort that could take vital signs continuously – the sort only rich people and private hospitals could afford. And aliens, apparently, or at least whack jobs who liked to colour their skin purple so they looked like aliens. His scrubs had ridden up, so she could see his skin was purple all the way down, not just his face. Weirdo.

She heaved the rest of him onto the gurney, then used the restraints to strap him down, just in case he woke up. Even with her massive belly, she was pretty sure she weighed less than him, so the sedative wouldn't keep him out for long.

Rifling through the cupboards of the medbay, she found herself a set of scrubs, and some more sedative to keep him docile, just in case. Oh, and some spray-on bandage so she could take that needle out of his neck and stem the bleeding. She dressed quickly, then pulled the syringe out. He didn't even wake when the bandage hit his skin, and she knew from experience that stuff stung. He'd meant to knock her out for a while, then.

She wanted to shake him awake and ask him what in the universe he'd thought he was doing to her. Nothing good, that's for sure.

Maia sighed. Whatever it was, she was free now, and he was her prisoner. That had to count for something. But first, she should get a feel for her surroundings, maybe call the police or something. Yes. That would be sensible. She found an injector gun, and loaded it with sedative. Six doses, for men like the Purple Prick here. Maybe seven if she had to shoot someone her size.

She hoped she wouldn't have to shoot anyone. She'd probably miss, unless it was at point blank range, or whatever you called it when you held a weapon to someone's skin. She was a nurse, not a soldier.

Gripping the injector in both hands, she headed out of the medbay.

Whoever this whack job was, he could certainly afford expensive toys. Sleek, gleaming walls greeted her at every turn, and the seats in his lounge area looked like real leather. She stepped into what could only be called a cockpit and her heart sank. She was in space, judging by how that moon was growing bigger and bigger in the viewscreen. Maybe he was an alien and not a whack job after all.

No, he was an alien whack job, and that was that.

She'd done a cursory search of the living quarters, then a quick glance into the cavernous cargo bay, before she came to the conclusion that she was alone with him on the ship. Well, that made things simpler.

The gurney had a hover capability, which made it easy for her to push all the way from the medbay to the airlock. It could even decant him onto the floor, like a load of dirty laundry. She particularly liked that function.

Gritting her teeth, she dragged the gurney back out in the corridor and closed the airlock, with the alien inside. Then she engaged the manual lock, so he couldn't get out, and sat down to wait.

Loud clanging woke her from her unplanned nap, followed by some particularly colourful swearing. So she had successfully locked him in, then, and he didn't have some secret way out she hadn't been able to find.

She peeked through the little view window. The restraints still held him, and from all the flailing about like a fresh-caught fish, it sounded like he liked being held captive even less than she did. Ah, but he'd spied her, and she was pretty sure fish couldn't feel the sort of fury she saw on his face.

"Foolish woman, I demand you release me

immediately, or you'll regret it!" he shouted.

Maia cocked her head to the side. "Mm, no, I don't think I will, thanks. I feel much safer with this big, thick airlock door between us."

He began to struggle again. "Foolish girl! You don't understand. If you don't release me right now, both you and the specimen will die!"

So he wasn't calling her a specimen – he was referring to whatever made her belly so round. Maia's breath caught in her throat at the thought of some alien larva bursting out of her.

"What did you put in me, you prick?" she demanded, before realising that she might have answered her own question. He was an alien, and she did look pregnant…

"You carry within you a child that combines the best of our two species. If he but survives the birth, he will be a god among men. Now, you must release me so I can remove him, before your weak form expires like the other, inferior hosts."

Fury flooded her veins. This arsehole had not only raped and impregnated her, but he'd done the same to other women, before he'd killed them. He deserved to be cut up into little pieces – while he was still alive, of course – and forced to watch them being fed to some primitive predator. A shark, maybe. If only there was a shark tank aboard, but she hadn't seen one. Probably for the best. It'd be a lot of effort and she wasn't sure this arsewipe was worth it.

"We have a name for things like you," she spat. "Psychopath. Or serial killer. Either way, it sounds like the universe will be a better place if I release you out the airlock."

"My name is Kronos, foolish girl, and I am a genius! My experiments will create a super race, formed of Titan and Human, who will rule the universe!"

Maia wasn't sure whether to laugh or cry. Super villain, much?

"Release me, and I will grant you the honour of bearing more of my master race.

Generations hence, they will worship you as their mother goddess!"

Being kept in a prison and forced to become a brood mare for this psycho's children? In what universe was that something she could possibly want?

"Sounds like I'll be doing the universe a favour, Purple People Eater," she said, slamming her clenched fist down on the manual release for the outer door.

He let out another stream of curses, higher pitched this time as he started to panic, before he was swept out into space.

Maybe it made her a bit of a psychopath, too, but Maia couldn't bring herself to regret ridding the universe of one more entitled arsehole. Besides, she had her own problems to deal with, she thought as she glanced down. There was definitely movement in her belly, which couldn't be good.

Time to call an ambulance or the police, if there was such a thing as emergency services in space. Call for help from someone, anyway.

And when help was on the way, she'd head back to the medbay and do some scans on herself and her…passenger.

TWO

"No," Nihal said.

Ghost spread his arms wide. "Is that any way to greet your only brother? What would your boss say if he knew you were turning away good customers?"

Nihal yanked a tray of glasses out of the dishwasher and began to put them away. "Vulcan knows as well as I do that you've never been and never will be a paying customer in this place. You only drink cheap beer, and we don't serve that here. You only come in here when you want a favour from me. Last time, you asked me to pick colour schemes for your new house. I nearly went cross eyed, trying to tell the difference between dove grey and mist, or a hundred different shades of white, to pick the perfect one, only to get a completely different palette for the next room. So whatever it is you want, the answer is no."

Ghost knew she couldn't really be serious. They were all the family each other had. "Come on, you know you wanted to decorate my house. I'd have picked one colour and done the whole house in that. See? I saw that shudder. You liked picking out all those colours. But this isn't about my new house. If I can get you to chance your no into a yes, will you give me a drink of the good stuff?"

She sniffed. "That depends. Are you on call tonight?"

Ghost winced. "Yes, but we both know the callout won't come on Christmas Eve. It'll be tomorrow, when we sit down to lunch or dinner. Besides, I've told you before, the alcohol evaporates when I dematerialise. When I arrive where I'm needed and reassemble myself, I'm as sober as the next man."

As if he was secretly trying to prove Nihal's point, the man next to Ghost slipped off his bar stool and crashed to the floor, knocking himself out. The fresh cocktail he'd held in his hand splashed everywhere, soaking Ghost's pants.

The scent of fruit syrup and potent spirits wafted up. Ghost wrinkled his nose.

"I'm not serving alcohol to Emergency Services personnel who are on duty. If you got called in and your slow reflexes got someone killed, I'd never forgive myself," Nihal said. "I'll bet you a virgin mojito you won't change my mind, which means if I win, you buy that drink for me." She grinned.

Ooh, she was twisty. No wonder she was a water djinn, while he was master of the whirlwind instead.

"Deal," Ghost said.

She turned away from him to serve a couple of customers, before she was back. "All right. What is it you want, brother mine?"

"You remember that aircar accident in the tunnels to Nyx last week?"

Nihal frowned. "That was nasty. Didn't a bunch of people end up in hospital? The tunnel was closed for hours — some of our patrons couldn't get home. Did you have to do the cleanup for that?" Something in her expression started to soften.

"I was the first on the scene. The other guys needed to get into their EV suits, but you know me — I head straight in, naked, no suit needed. One aircar had crashed into the other, shattering several of the windows. Rapid decompression and loss of atmosphere, plus damage to the ventilation units, meant a carload of people got decompression sickness, before the safety systems kicked in and sealed the holes. First thing I did was turn up the oxygen levels to maximum, which helped. But one passenger, he was just a kid, a teenager, he had heart problems. That's all he managed to tell me before he passed out. Because I was there first, I could relay to the others we needed emergency evac for him first, and he survived. Wanted to see me today to thank me, in fact. Said I'd saved his life." Ghost grinned. It wasn't often he got to be a hero, but it was an awesome feeling. That was what kept him going, even when his search and rescue callouts didn't have such happy endings.

"So you're a hero. You do a lot of good in Emergency Services, Ghost. Don't let anyone tell you different."

Ghost managed to keep the smile on his face, but it was hard. He didn't want to tell Nihal that he couldn't remember a week when someone hadn't screamed at him for failing to save their partner/child/pet/prized possession when nothing short of a miracle would've saved them, and maybe not even that. Those last days on Tito, when the robot rebellion destroyed half the city, he'd had people screaming at him, blaming him for the deaths he'd arrived too late to prevent. Some of them had actually expected him to run out in front of the robots and get killed trying to retrieve their loved one's corpse. It had been a special kind of hell, working in Emergency Services back then. So for every time he fought fate and failed…it was nice to have the occasional victory. Especially as there were no robots in the Colony at all.

The Colony was also the only place in the whole Altan system with cocoa beans, though the first crop had been very small, and bought in its entirety by one business owner. "Do you know a café owner called Dulcinea?" Ghost asked.

Nihal's eyes widened. "You mean the woman who owns the Chocolaterie? She comes in here occasionally. She's quite partial to our pomegranate fizz, especially now we can get real pomegranates to garnish the glass."

Ghost nodded. "That's her. Well, the owner of the Chocolaterie, anyway — I don't know what she normally drinks. I do know that she's the relieved mother of Pollux, a teenage boy who's lucky to be alive right now. Relieved and so grateful, in fact, that she said I could come in and choose my favourites to fill her biggest box of truffles to take home. Seeing as you like chocolate so much and your taste is oh so much better than mine…" He suppressed a grin when he saw she at least had the grace to blush. "Well, I thought what better Christmas present for my favourite sister than to ask you to make the selection, so you can enjoy all those chocolates?"

Nihal leaped over the bar and wrapped him in a tight hug. "Yes! A thousand times yes! You are the best brother, Ghost!"

He waited for her to get back behind the bar before he said, "See? I knew you'd say yes. So, does that mean I get that drink? Some sort of virgin, you said?"

Nihal raised her eyebrows. "I didn't think you were into virgins of any kind."

Now it was Ghost's turn to blush. Of

course his sister knew he was attracted to women who were a little more experienced, who hadn't lived the most sheltered lives. Stars knew neither of them had been particularly sheltered, even on Titan. Ghost had gotten his taste for cheap beer when that's the best he could afford, and drinking the more expensive stuff seemed like forgetting where he'd come from.

But this wasn't about women. "Make me my drink, woman," he growled.

"If you weren't giving me a big box of chocolates tomorrow, I'd box your ears for that," Nihal said. She reached into the fridge and pulled out a jar of leaves, then plucked several out of the jar.

Ghost couldn't remember the last time he'd smelled fresh mint.

Nihal smiled. "Wait until you taste the syrup. From real Colony honey, harvested in the Ager Dome. The lime juice is still from concentrate, but I hear we'll have our first citrus harvest in a few short months, so it's not long to wait now."

As Ghost watched, she assembled the cocktail, layer by layer, until she reached for the leaf jar again to pluck one more sprig of mint. "For my hero of a brother, who gives the best – "

His comm buzzed.

Ghost's heart tightened in his chest as he read the message. "I'm needed at work. Sorry, sis, I have to go." He gave the drink one last, longing look, before heading for the door.

"I'll put in the fridge for you!" she called after him.

"I'll be back for it!" he called back.

Or so he thought.

THREE

Maia slammed her fist into the console. "That's it. Next time I do the universe a favour, I'm going to get the psychopath's passwords out of him first, before I space him. Or maybe I should've cut some bits off – just his hand, so I could use it on the scanner." She glared at the blinking scanner.

None of this could help her now, though. Kronos or whatever his name was had locked her out of the ship's computer system, so she couldn't view or change the ship's course, or switch on the comm to call for help.

The only thing she could do was set off the distress beacon, because the controls on those were so simple an overtired toddler could activate it. Just one big, red button, under a lift-up cover, so no one pressed it by accident.

Then again, if she did activate it, who was to say that more purple alien arsewipes would home in on her, and maybe do worse things than whatever Kronos had planned?

Better to do that full medical scan, so she'd at least know what her future held. Imminent death, unplanned motherhood, or something she hadn't considered yet? Whatever it was, it wouldn't make her current situation any worse to know more about it.

Besides, if she only had hours to live, she'd like a chance to write a letter to her family, or a note for whoever found her body, before searching this ship for enough alcohol to make those last few hours pass comfortably.

She'd dragged the high tech gurney back to

the medbay, so that's where she bent her steps. Unhooking the tablet that evidently controlled the gurney's higher functions, she climbed up onto the bed and instructed it to perform a full health scan. Good thing Kronos hadn't thought to lock this system, too, or maybe she simply hadn't given him a chance to, as he was using it at the time when she stabbed him with the syringe.

"Please relax and remain still," the tablet intoned.

Maia set the tablet on the mattress beside her and tried to obey its orders.

After a long moment, the tablet announced, "Scan complete."

Maia snatched it up, scrolling through the data. Heartbeat, blood pressure, oxygen levels – all normal. She flipped ahead to the section where health alerts were listed. There was only one alert: a great big caution notice that the patient had a near-term pregnancy, therefore certain procedures and tests should not be performed, but several further scans were recommended.

Maia ticked them all, then pressed the START button.

Once again, the tablet ordered her to hold still.

This time, the wait seemed longer.

Maia hadn't planned a pregnancy yet – she'd hoped to have found someone to co-parent with before she considered children. To be fair, she'd hoped to have finished her stint in space medicine, to complement her nursing and midwifery qualifications, so she could apply for a cushy colony job. Granted, being assigned to the *Genesis* was a coup she'd scarcely dreamed of pulling off, but after the terrorist attack, she'd been stuck in the right place and the right time to be offered a stasis pod on the most well-funded colony expedition ever to leave Earth.

Instead of delivering babies for rich trophy wives, though, she'd been reassigned as a field medic on the *Magellan*, one of the exploration vessels that had been conscripted as a scout ship when the war started, and she was willing to bet she now knew more about space combat wounds than her instructors back on Earth. She could remember her last shift so clearly. She'd been doing routine health checks on the crew, before the battle stations alarm had sounded. That meant all the crew had other places to be, and her job was to be well-rested and ready when casualties came in. That meant tucking herself into one of the empty lifepods in the break room, and grabbing a nap until she was needed.

Lifepods that automatically shut to protect the occupant if there was a hull breach or the command was given to abandon ship, because they were supposed to be for patients. So if something had happened to the ship, and she'd been put into emergency stasis in the lifepod, she could have floated in space for who knew how long before Kronos had found her to use in his breeding experiment. Or worse, some salvager had found her and sold her to Kronos…

Maia suppressed a shudder at the thought of her unconscious body being trafficked through who knew how many unknown hands before she'd wound up in her present predicament. Human trafficking was illegal, or at least it had been. How far into the future had her pod drifted before she'd been found? Long enough for men to revert to primitive barbarism where space cowboys did what they pleased?

Yet if this ship and the gurney were any indication, technology hadn't advanced or regressed that much. Why, the ship looked almost new, which meant there was still an advanced civilisation somewhere. Hopefully within reach of her distress beacon, when she activated it…

The tablet informed her that the additional scans were complete. Within her womb, she carried a healthy baby boy of estimated weight 3.8 kilograms, perfectly positioned for a natural birth. There were even pictures of the mite — oh, he was sucking his tiny thumb!

Maia took a deep breath, then blew it out,

trying to think like a midwife and not a soon-to-be mum. She'd likely go into labour in the next few days, with a high likelihood of a normal birth without complications. She could induce the labour, and help it progress faster, so she'd be less exhausted and more capable of handling the birth on her own, unassisted. That was better for the baby, too.

Of course, if there were complications, she'd be in no place to do anything about them, without someone to help. Both she and the child could die, and no one would ever know why.

She slid off the gurney and headed for the cockpit, or whatever the place with the flight controls was called on a ship like this. On the *Magellan*, they'd called it a bridge, but they'd had various different displays manned by a whole team of people, not a control panel with seats for a pilot and a copilot.

She flipped up the cover and pressed her palm to the button. If this summoned help, she'd buy everyone drinks or bake everyone cookies, if such things existed out here.

If it summoned more trouble, she had a fully loaded injector gun and she was particularly partial to stabbing men in the arse with it.

"Distress beacon activated," the ship told her with the calm only artificial intelligence could muster.

Fingers crossed help arrived before any actual distress. Or she'd be forced to start shooting.

FOUR

He'd only taken two steps into the Emergency Services control centre, but he already knew it was going to be bad. Fallon's frown confirmed it – just seeing her in the control centre after hours was a harbinger of some coming apocalypse, or at least an incident with multiple casualties. She was the only incident controller qualified to take charge when things got really bad.

Ghost said a silent prayer to the universe

that this one didn't involve robots, or children in danger. Everyone in the unit had their post traumatic stress triggers, and those were his.

"What's up, boss?" he asked.

Fallon might be the harbinger of the apocalypse, but she was a breeze to work for. No standing on ceremony, just acting on orders and doing what needed to be done.

"An asteroid miner found the remains of a wreck. Likely shot down during the war. It seemed like a standard salvage operation, until they found occupied stasis pods in the debris. Some of them were damaged, and the mining ship doesn't have the right medical facilities to handle pulling potentially injured people out of stasis. We're sending a team in to assess the situation and escort the pods here."

Ghost scanned the screens Fallon couldn't take her eyes off.

"Looks like a scout ship. Not new, either — could be Human or Titan, picked up as part of the evacuation and parked in a colony ship's hold until arrival. Hiding out in the asteroid belt, I'd bet on civilians, mining for supplies, likely with their families along," Ghost said. His heart sank.

Fallon nodded. "Could be. We won't know until we start cracking the pods. That's why I sent a stasis tech out with our team."

The team had already gone, without him. Not unusual, because Ghost could get there faster than any ship, but he dared to hope. "Want me to go out there and take a look?" he asked.

Fallon shook her head slowly, eyes still glued to the screen. "We have eyes out there already. The mining ship crew are seasoned — all experienced with EV operations. I need you to deal with a distress call that just came in." She pulled a new picture onto the screen. "The *Burro*, listed as a cargo hauler, presumed lost during the war, but it looks like a brand new space yacht to me. Currently on a course for New Hope's moon, though it's anyone's guess why. Maybe they intended to come here instead, but they developed an engine fault.

Some sort of fault, anyway, because they're not answering comms. If they don't correct course, they will crash into the moon. Think you can head out there and check it out for me?"

Ghost grinned. "My guess is the rich bastard who owns the yacht was getting busy with his current mistress on the control panel, and she kicked the distress beacon by accident. By the time I reach them, they'll be done and the course correction will be already in the works."

"Bet you dinner they're still at it when you get there, and you get an eyeful that you won't be able to get out of your head for days. I'll bet you drinks, too, if you can find a single fault with her. Physically, I mean."

"Deal." Not that he needed another dinner and drinks at her expense — he still hadn't collected on the last bet he'd won. Dinner and drinks for two…maybe he'd take Nihal out for Christmas dinner tomorrow, when he returned from this callout. Because there was no way Fallon would win this bet.

"Oh, and leave your clothes in the change

room like a normal person. Last time, your undies ended up on my desk, and I had a meeting with the Watch Commander that morning!"

Ghost sketched a salute. "Sure, boss." They hadn't even been his undies – he suspected one of the other guys had done it as a joke – but until he knew who it was, it wasn't worth arguing about.

He headed for the change room, and stripped off, laying his ordinary underwear on top of the rest of his uniform in his locker. How Fallon believed the skimpy, glittery briefs she'd found could ever belong to him, he wasn't sure.

A mystery to solve some other day, he told himself, as his body shed its matter and became the whirlwind, like the kama itachi he was. A creature who could ride the solar winds through the vacuum, no cumbersome space suit required.

He'd be aboard the *Burro* in no time, and back in the Colony before he knew it.

FIVE

Maia needed a nap, but she needed nourishment, too. Whether the alien had stocked the galley with anything resembling food, well, that was another matter. If he hadn't, she'd have to use some of the nutrient packs in the medbay and hook up an IV line. There might be thousands of ways to die in space, but Maia was not going to give in to something as common as starvation.

No, she'd likely die birthing this alien baby.

But not before she'd eaten dinner, she swore.

The first few cupboards she opened contained nothing but alcohol – the good stuff, top shelf only, and all from Earth. Had Kronos stolen this ship from its unsuspecting Human owner? Maia wouldn't have put it past him. Perhaps throwing him out the airlock had been more merciful than he deserved, seeing as he'd likely done the same to the ship's owner.

Maia shuddered, and not from the cool air pooling at her feet from the open cabinet. They were climate controlled – nice! If Kronos had cared enough about his stolen Earth booze to refrigerate it, then surely there'd be something edible in here somewhere.

Four cabinets later, she hit the jackpot – shelves full of boxes labelled PRET A MANGER, which her high school language lessons told her meant ready to eat. Just like her, she thought, tugging out the nearest box.

She laid it on the counter, then ripped the tape off with her fingernails, too impatient to find a knife.

The tape came away with most of the lettering, so now the box only said MANGER, which is exactly what she hoped to do with the contents.

She'd expected ration bars, or something dehydrated, but instead she found vacuum packed lobster in some sort of sauce. Luckily, the instructions came in several languages, so she unwrapped the top tray, put it in the heating unit and set the temperature and timer.

While her meal cooked, she searched through the cabinets for something to drink. No alcohol, of course, but she hoped for a fruit-flavoured nutrient drink, like they'd served in the mess aboard the *Magellan*. Once again, the ship's owner surprised her with a selection of fruit juices.

Maia cracked a can of what promised to be apple and strawberry juice, and sipped the stuff straight from the can. Ambrosia, surely – the strawberries tasted like they'd been picked yesterday, without a hint of artificial flavour syrup or added sugar. She could live on the contents of this kitchen forever…or at least as long as supplies lasted. No, she wouldn't starve.

She'd finished the can of juice by the time the heating unit chimed to tell her that her lobster was ready, so she grabbed a second can of juice to wash down her meal. If she survived the birth, she'd open a bottle of wine, she promised herself.

Right now, she toasted the first real lobster she'd ever eaten with white grape juice, and hoped her luck would hold long enough to deliver help on the way, and a safe birth.

SIX

The Burro looked fine on the outside – no hull damage or unusual radiation emissions. If it weren't for the pulsing distress beacon and kamikaze course, Ghost wouldn't have looked twice at the space yacht, for that's definitely what this beauty was. Cargo ship, indeed.

He bypassed the airlock and slipped though the gaps in the ship's radiation shielding, swimming through the current in the wiring until he took form in the cockpit. The deserted cockpit.

Ghost punched the air in triumph. He'd already won his bet with Fallon. Christmas dinner was sorted.

He pressed his palm to the reader, but the control panel didn't recognise his imprint. Ghost cursed. Every ship in the system was supposed to respond to an authorised Emergency Services agent. Luckily, he was a being of both energy and matter, and he could tickle the sensors until…bingo.

The viewscreen lit up with status displays, framing the view of New Hope's moon, which the display had helpfully labelled as Endor.

Ghost shrugged. Someone must have named the moon, so Endor must have meant something important to someone.

Now he could see the charted course, the *Burro* really was headed into lunar orbit on the dark side of Endor. Hiding from someone, obviously, but whether they'd intended to rendezvous with someone to transfer a cargo of contraband, attack the Colony, or something entirely harmless, Ghost didn't know.

What he could see was that there was nothing wrong with the ship – not a warning to be seen.

Let Fallon or someone else figure it out.

He opened a comm channel with the control room and slipped on a headset. "Colony Control, this is Ghost on the *Burro*, over."

"Sitrep, Ghost. Over."

"The ship seems fine. Nothing wrong with the engines, hull, radiation levels, air quality…the only thing that seems slightly suspicious is the charted course – into orbit on the dark side of New Hope's moon, staying out of radar range of the Colony the whole way. Er, over."

"Confirm, Ghost. Charted course is to New Hope or Endor orbit?"

Ghost almost laughed. Fallon knew the name of the moon? Of course she did. It must be some strange Human reference.

"Endor. You got anything else on radar out there?"

"Negative, Ghost, but I'll get someone on it. Could be stealthed. Any survivors?"

"None that I've seen on the flight deck. I haven't left the cockpit, though."

"Someone set off the distress beacon, Ghost. Report back when you've done a more thorough check. Out."

The comm went silent.

Ghost swore under his breath. He wasn't normally this stupid. He could search the ship, or he could get the computer to do it for him. He swiped a hand across the console, commanding it to scan the ship for life signs.

He waited a moment, before an image of the ship appeared onscreen. The only heat signature was his own, in the cockpit. The ship was empty.

Where had everybody gone?

Wait, what was that?

He blinked, but the image looked the same. Yet for a moment there, he thought he'd seen the red spot in the cockpit move.

Must have imagined it.

What he didn't imagine was the sharp pain in his neck, or the darkness that followed.

He didn't even have time to swear.

SEVEN

It was a male voice that woke Maia – one she definitely didn't recognise. She shouldn't have eaten that second portion of lobster, but it had been so good…before it put her into a sort of food coma on the soft leather couches in the galley. She should have done a more thorough search of the ship, if she'd missed a second man. Alien. Arsehole. Whatever.

Good thing she still had the injector gun. This guy was going down.

She followed the sound of his voice until she reached the cockpit. He'd managed to unlock the control panel, which meant he was undoubtedly part of this ship's crew. He had that same lavender shade to his skin, too, so he was definitely an alien. Kronos's accomplice, who deserved a similar fate, she was sure of it.

He certainly had a foul enough vocabulary as he tapped on the console, commanding the computer to bring up some sort of schematic of the ship.

She got as close as she dared, then took advantage of his distraction to fire off a shot from her injector gun. The first dart missed, so she stepped closer. The second one sank into his neck.

He crumpled to the deck.

It took her longer to manoeuvre the second man onto the gurney and into the airlock, partially because she'd forced herself to stop for a sheet to cover his nakedness — he wasn't wearing a skin-coloured coverall, as she'd thought, but his own purple skin. He might be about to die, but he deserved to preserve a little bit of modesty in his final moments.

She let him keep the sheet in the airlock, too. She had plenty in the medbay – she wouldn't miss it. Besides, she hadn't found anywhere to wash it yet, and she'd have to be pretty desperate to use a sheet that had last been up close and personal to some alien's privates. Aliens who should've been able to find love or at least the physical approximation of it with someone willing, if they were all as well-endowed as Number Two here. Then again, maybe they were all crazy, entitled arseholes like Kronos.

Not that she'd looked at his privates, aside from a glance when she'd realised he was naked. No, ogling aliens was definitely not a good idea.

So now, for the second time, she stood outside the airlock, waiting for an alien to wake up. This time, she'd measured the dose of sedative, so she knew he'd soon be stirring. Almost to the minute, she thought with satisfaction, as he stood up.

Maia squeezed her eyes shut, but not before she'd gotten an eyeful. Stars, she did not need to know the alien had a perfect arse. Like a pair of gibbous moons…but with dimples!

Aliens had no business having dimples.

"Give me one good reason why I shouldn't throw you out the airlock right now," she said to his…back. "What did you do to me?"

He spun on the spot, then caught sight of her in the view window.

Thankfully, he reached down for the sheet and used it to cover things before he spoke.

"Ma'am, I didn't know you existed until you stabbed me with whatever you used to knock me out." He frowned as he rubbed his neck. "I have done nothing to you, and I have no intention of doing anything to you. I came to investigate your distress beacon."

It must have set off some sort of alarm inside the ship, which had brought him out of his hiding place. An alarm only aliens could hear, because she hadn't heard anything.

"Right, when you're a purple alien, just like he was. Where were you hiding?" she demanded. "Are you the ship's engineer or something, that you didn't know what he was doing to me?"

"What who was doing to you, ma'am? If someone aboard has hurt you, I promise he'll face justice for his crimes. If you tell me where he is, I'll see that he's suitably restrained so that he can't hurt you any more. Are you injured? Do you require medical assistance?"

Stars help her, but he sounded like her, processing some assault victim in the Emergency Department back on Earth. She glanced down at her swollen belly. Yes, she did need medical assistance, but not from some stars-crossed purple alien.

"Who are you? Where were you hiding on the ship? Is there anyone else aboard?" she asked.

He'd fashioned the sheet into a sort of loincloth. Almost like he had a fair amount of practice at such things. It meant he could raise both hands in the air, like he was surrendering. "Ma'am, I'm Agent Ghost from Colony Emergency Services. I came to investigate your distress call. I don't know if there is anyone else aboard this vessel, as you're the only person I've seen so far. As I've already stated, if anyone here has hurt you, I'm authorised to take a preliminary report from you and place the offender under temporary arrest until we reach our destination. If you'll only let me out of this airlock, so I can better assist you."

She wanted to believe him. Truly, she did. If that was all true, she could let him search the ship, and navigate her to somewhere with decent medical care and maybe even a qualified obstetrician. She'd settle for a moderately experienced midwife.

But he was a purple alien, and she knew better than to trust them.

"Where's your ship, then? Or your shuttle? What about your space suit?"

He ducked his head. "Ma'am, I'm an EV specialist, working mostly in vacuum, trained to operate without a support vehicle or other safety equipment…"

He was lying. He had to be. No one could survive in space without even a space suit!

"Prove it, then," she said, and hit the button that opened the outer airlock doors.

"Wait, ma'am, please, wait!"

Swallowing, she turned away. She didn't want to watch this one die.

EIGHT

Ghost's body hit vacuum and he could only swear inwardly as his body lost integrity and disintegrated.

Well, that had gone well. The guys back in the office would laugh their heads off at him when they read the report on this one. He almost wished he had walked in on an orgy in the cockpit. It would've been easier to live down.

He took a moment to gather his thoughts

before he decided what to do next.

There was one female inside the ship, possible assault victim, perpetrator unknown. His whereabouts unknown. Then again, he'd only seen that one – no, two – heat signatures in the cockpit, before she stabbed him. There hadn't been anyone else on the ship.

Unless her assailant was a Titan who didn't have a normal heat signature. He'd have to search the ship himself to be certain, and without being seen by her assailant.

So his first task was the one Fallon had given him – search the ship for signs of life. Neutralise any threat said life forms posed. Assess the woman's injuries. Then, take corporeal form and report back to base.

He flew a search pattern, then did it again, just to be sure. Both times, he found only one person aboard the *Burro* – one angry, very pregnant woman in a set of surgical scrubs.

Perhaps he should report to Fallon first, THEN try to calm the woman down, because there was no way she was going to allow him to assess her injuries if she'd mistaken him for some other arsehole. A purple arsehole, if he remembered correctly. Perhaps he should try a different colour. In his experience, purple usually had a calming effect on people. Maybe he should try green.

Ah, but she was Human, wasn't she? Perhaps he should go with a more Human shade of brown, and clothes. Maybe she was from one of those prudish Earth cultures that objected to nudity. Or maybe she was just like most people, who freaked out and did irrational things in a disaster. Though throwing him out an airlock was a new one, even for him.

Ghost sighed. First, he had to see that the woman was safe, before reporting to Fallon. Which meant negotiation skills while wearing dirty overalls. Unless there was a set of scrubs in his size somewhere…

When he headed for the galley, where he knew the pregnant woman was, he wore green scrubs over Human-coloured skin. She couldn't possibly mistake him for whoever had hurt her now.

A mystery man who was no longer aboard the ship.

Had she shoved him out the airlock, too?

Gutsy move for a pregnant girl. Ghost found himself grinning. He could almost like her, if she hadn't tried to kill him and all.

Yeah, there was that. Attempted murder was something he was supposed to report. Something else he could worry about later, when he had to comm Fallon. Yet another reason he should wait.

First, he had to build enough trust with the girl so he could assess her injuries.

He cleared his throat as he entered the galley, just in case she hadn't heard his footsteps. Then he held up his hands and sidled away from the doorway, giving her an easy exit. "Ma'am, I just need to ask you a few questions," he began.

She shot up out of her seat and pointed what looked like an injector gun at him. Ah, so that's how she'd stabbed him – she'd shot him. Clever.

"Please put the gun down, ma'am. Like I said, I'm from Colony Emergency Services, and I'm here to help you. I can't do that if I'm unconscious, or if you throw me out the airlock again."

"You…why aren't you dead? Does that mean the other one isn't dead, either?" Her hands, and the gun with them, trembled.

"I'm a trained specialist, ma'am. I'm one of the few agents who can operate in a vacuum without needing transport or a suit."

"That's not possible."

"I assure you, ma'am, it is. I'm a kama itachi, which is a kind of djinn."

"You're one of the aliens we're at war with! A Titan!"

Pity smote him hard. How long had she been held captive on this ship? Long enough to get pregnant, presumably, but the war had ended more than three years ago. "The war is over, ma'am. Humans and Titans signed a peace treaty, and now share the Colony on New Hope, where I live when I'm not out in space, answering distress calls." He wanted to say more, but his training made him hold his tongue. This wasn't the time for sarcastic comments.

"What system is this? And what planet is your New Hope?"

"We're in the Altan system, ma'am, and New Hope is the seventh planet from the sun. The first three planets – Beta, Gamma and Delta – belong to the Titans, and the other three – Elysium, Styx and Gaia, I believe they're called – are Human planets. New Hope is the only neutral planet, where we live in peace in the Colony." He recalled the last couple of callouts he'd had inside the Colony. "Well, mostly in peace. Some arseholes would start a war with their own shoes just for something to fight."

She lifted her head, her eyes begging for something he suspected he couldn't give. "I don't suppose there's a hospital in your

Colony, is there? With all the latest in medical technology?"

"Yes, ma'am, there is. The best medical facility in the Altan system is right down on the surface of New Hope. Under the Colony dome, in Metropolis City."

"There are no cities in the Altan system. At least, there weren't…"

Instead of giving her comfort, he'd freaked her out again. Stars, he sucked at negotiating. Maybe that's why he got yelled at so much.

"It was built at the end of the war. A joint project between Humans and Titans." But mostly Humans, because the *Genesis* had been full of the construction crew who built the ship, tradespeople with the necessary experience. There had been a few Titans there, though. Allie, for one. It was her presence on the construction crew and her assurance that she'd be living in the Colony that had given him and a whole lot of others the confidence to become First Settlers.

She'd closed her eyes, squeezing them shut

as if his words hurt her. A long moment passed, before her eyes popped open again. "Take me there," she said.

"Yes, ma'am," Ghost said, relieved. "What shall I tell the hospital about your injuries?"

She let out a breathy laugh. "Tell them I've just gone into labour, and stars only know what sort of alien baby that prick put inside me while I was unconscious." She doubled over, clutching at her belly.

Ghost felt all the blood drain from his face as he swore. "Are you serious?"

"As a supernova."

Swearing some more, Ghost raced for the cockpit.

NINE

Maia blew out a breath and straightened. Braxton Hicks contractions were a nuisance, but they were bearable. At least she wasn't really in labour yet. Those contractions would be much worse. All the more reason to know more about this man and where he'd come from, if he hadn't been aboard the ship, helping Kronos.

She heaved herself out of the chair and headed after the chameleon alien. Whoever he was going to communicate with, she wanted to hear every word.

"Colony Control? This is Ghost on the Burro. I have your sitrep."

Ghost was his name, she remembered, and was this ship called the Burro? Huh. It fit. Butter, to go with the boxes of lobster in the galley.

"One survivor aboard the ship. Injuries unknown, but she's in labour. Request immediate permission to land."

"What's that, Ghost? You're breaking up."

"Must be the moon, blocking the signal. I said I have an injured woman in labour. Having a baby. Need to land now. Have a medevac team ready."

"Can't…land. There's no room at the…" A burst of static erupted from the console. "In…"

"Please repeat that, Control. You said there's no room at the inn?" Ghost said.

"Cargo bay…full. Mining ship…blocked…no entrance. Will

clear...can...." More crackling. "Can you stay...stable?"

"You want me to what? Stay in a stable? I have a woman in labour. Medical emergency. With a baby." Unlike in the galley, Ghost definitely didn't sound calm any more. There was a definite edge of panic in his tone.

Maybe she should come clean, and tell him she wasn't actually in labour yet.

"Stars, Ghost, just get into a stable orbit and hold your position. The mining ship beat you here, and we're using every aerobridge in the cargo bay to evacuate people from damaged stasis pods. Wait your turn. I'll update you in twelve hours. Fallon, out."

Ghost buried his head in his hands.

Maia stepped forward, not sure what to say, but certain she had to say something. Then another of those stupid, fake contractions seized her, as something warm trickled down her leg.

Great blithering black holes. Now was not the time for her waters to break. So much for

Braxton Hicks – these contractions were about to get very real, and very painful.

"Um, Mr Ghost, I'm going to need your help getting to the medbay. This baby doesn't want to wait."

Maia wanted to be wrong, but she was an experienced enough midwife to know she wasn't.

Ghost straightened. "Sure thing, ma'am. Don't you worry at all. Everything's going to be fine."

She'd liked it better when she was the one lying.

TEN

They had to stop twice while she doubled over for contractions before they made it to the medbay. Ghost tried to stave off panic by racking his brains to remember his first aid training in dealing with women in labour. The only part he remembered was keeping them calm until they could get to a hospital, because traumatic events often brought on early labour, and injuries complicated things. He didn't know what to do when he was stuck out in space, no hospital in sight, with not the slightest clue how to birth a baby.

He helped her onto the hospital bed, then scanned the room, searching for something that might let him access the information he needed. Surely there was a tablet or some other way to tap into the ship's computer. Every vessel was required to keep a first aid manual on file, both Human and Titan. It was like a distress beacon. You didn't leave atmosphere without it.

"Commencing scan," said a voice that definitely didn't belong to the woman.

Ghost whirled, to find she held a tablet in her hands. "Is there an AI on this ship?" he asked.

She shrugged. "Not that I know of. Just a computer that talks and responds to voice commands, because it's too hard to properly disinfect your hands if you have to keep touching the screen all the time during a procedure."

"Scan complete. Patient is three centimetres

dilated, mother and baby heartbeats are both normal. Estimated time of arrival…"

She shook her head at the tablet. "No. That'll take too long. Mr Ghost, can you check in the cupboards for some oxytocin? I'm sure I saw some earlier. Oh, wait, I left it on the counter. There!" She pointed. "Hand me the vial and the dish beside it, please."

Ghost was familiar with plenty of drugs, but this wasn't one of them. "What does it do?" he asked as he picked up the items.

He had to wait while she tensed up through a contraction before she said, "It'll speed this up. I don't want to still be in labour during reentry." She gritted her teeth through another contraction.

"But…surely pain relief would be better. Or waiting until we land…" Ghost began.

She laughed through gritted teeth. "This baby wants out now, and the only way to stop labour once it's started is to get the baby out. Unless you're a secret anaesthetist or qualified surgeon, the only way that's going to happen is the old fashioned way. Pain relief would be wonderful, but the only ones I'm qualified to administer will make me too dopey. So unless you're an expert at delivering babies, Mr Ghost, I suggest you just let me get on with things." With practiced ease, she ripped open the packaging, filled the syringe, then injected the contents into herself. She smoothed a little sticky dressing over the wound site, then thrust the dish full of rubbish at his chest. "Get rid of that, will you?"

A new contraction seized her, and Ghost turned away to search for somewhere to put the rubbish. By the time he'd found the disposal chute, she was panting as the pain ebbed. A brief respite.

"Ma'am, are you sure I shouldn't find you some pain relief?" Ghost asked. "Or I could try and raise a midwife at the hospital, to see if she can talk me through this. I've never birthed a baby before."

She laughed again. "Well, I've never given birth to one before, either, but you're in luck.

I've been on the catching side more times than I can count, so even if it's my first time throwing, I'll be calling the shots as long as I'm conscious, not some alien midwife I don't know."

It was on the tip of his tongue to tell her he didn't know if the Colony midwives were Human or Titan, but it wouldn't much matter. Not if comms between the *Burro* and Control were already acting up. "I might be able to help, if I could find some sort of manual…" he said instead.

"No manual can prepare you for your first birth, Mr Ghost, but I think there were a couple more medical tablets in that drawer over there." She pointed. "This one's mine, monitoring my vital signs and all."

"Yes, ma'am. Thank you, ma'am," Ghost said, sidling over to the drawer.

"Maia," she said. "My name is…Maia."

He ducked his head. "A pleasure to meet you, Maia, if in less than perfect circumstances. I'm Joost, though everyone calls me Ghost."

He held out his hand for her to shake.

Her grip was stronger than he expected, and that was before she squeezed his hand as she endured another contraction. "Is it too late to change my mind about that pain relief, Ghost?"

He waited until she released his hand before he pulled away. "I'll see what the manual says."

She let out a breathy laugh. "You do that. And if you find any laughing gas on the way, toss me a bottle. It'll take the edge off."

Cautiously, he asked, "Ah, could you remind me what that looks like?" Laughing gas sounded like the street name for the drug.

"Old hospitals on Earth had it piped to every room, so it was usually just a matter of turning on the tap, hooking up a mask, and you had as much as you need. Out here, and maybe on your planet, too, depending on how low the gravity is, inhalant anaesthesia isn't particularly practical, so....ungh!"

Ghost waited for the contraction to end, so Maia could finish.

She managed a weak smile. "It was a joke. You won't find nitrous here. Just a bunch of injectables."

A girl who could joke during a time like this…if he weren't so worried, Ghost might have fallen in love with her right then and there. Still might, if everything turned out okay. Because people who could laugh and keep calm during a disaster were few and far between.

Probably a good thing she was pregnant, and not likely to be looking for love any time soon. Speaking of which…

"Can I ask about the baby's father?" he said.

He had to wait until she relaxed before he got a reply.

"The alien who put this baby in me — no idea if he's the father or not, or even if the baby has my DNA…"

Another long wait, until she'd unclenched her teeth enough to talk.

"I found some medical records, indicating it was all done by IVF. Me and…"

She made a painful sound in the back of her throat.

"He did this to a whole bunch of women. It wasn't just me. The others…"

Stars, were there other women aboard this ship, too? They'd have to be in stasis, because he hadn't detected any life signs. He needed to contact Control – they'd have to let him land, with multiple casualties and all.

"The others didn't make it. Not sure if he was just incompetent or if something went wrong with the pregnancy or the birth. If I hadn't woken up…"

Ghost's heart constricted in his chest. How could she be so calm, talking about a long line of past murder victims, knowing she'd only narrowly avoided being the next? Maia deserved a medal.

"If I hadn't woken up, who knows how many more women he'd have forced to carry his engineered babies?"

How many indeed? If the man had still been here, Ghost wanted to space him himself.

"What happened to him?" Ghost asked. He figured he already knew, but he needed to hear her say it to be certain.

"I threw him out the airlock. Just like you, only he didn't come back. Yet. Can all aliens…?"

This time, he didn't wait for her to finish her sentence. "No, very few Titans can survive in a vacuum, and of those of us who can, only a handful can take Human form as well as an incorporeal one. I mean, there are air and water and earth elementals, who can switch between their element and a Human form, but only energy elementals can survive more than a few seconds in vacuum. So unless he was a fire elemental, or a kama itachi, like me, or one of the other creatures who use EM radiation for energy…you should be safe."

She relaxed, though whether from his words or the end of the contraction, he couldn't be sure.

Nodding, she reached for the tablet, which announced that it was doing another scan.

"Dilation at six centimetres. Estimated time of arrival..."

Maia turned pained eyes on him. "Do you think two hours are enough for you to read that manual you were talking about? Because..."

One look at her scrunched-up face and Ghost fancied he knew how much pain she was in. He didn't want to be her right now.

"Ma'am, I promise you, by the time your baby arrives, I will be an expert on anything childbirth related that's contained within the ship's database," Ghost said, waving the spare tablet he'd finally found in the right cupboard.

Maia smiled wanly, still panting. "Just don't faint on me, Ghost, and you'll be fine."

Somehow, he didn't think so, but he pasted a reassuring smile on his face and tried to look like he agreed with her. Of course, inside he was going to pieces like she'd thrown him out into the vacuum again. She probably would if he botched this birth, which, short of a miracle, was pretty much a certainty.

Was it wrong to hope for a miracle?

ELEVEN

Every contraction seemed to go on forever, until it was over, and then she barely had a moment to catch her breath before the next one crested. How women could actually want to go through labour without pain relief, she had no idea. If she ever had another baby, there'd be anaesthetic for days, or at least as long as she needed it.

In those brief, pain-free seconds, she instructed the tablet to scan her every fifteen minutes, until she reached full dilation, when the next stage of labour would begin. The riskiest part, and also the part where most men were worse than useless. Joost or Ghost or whatever he wanted to be called, well, he'd be no different when things got messy. She'd bet a whole box of lobster dinners he passed out before the baby was born.

She interrupted his reading to ask him to bring the wheeled table over to the bed, loaded with the instruments she'd laid out for the birth when she'd expected to endure this alone.

"Isn't there something I should be doing?" Ghost asked, eyeing her up and down.

Maia shook her head. "Mostly it's just moral support and keeping an eye on mum and baby's vitals, which are fine. The tablet will sound the alert if anything goes outside normal ranges."

He paled, looking almost as white as his namesake. Oh, he'd faint for sure. "What do I do if I hear the alert?"

She smiled grimly. "Do what I say, and

don't hesitate."

Fortunately, the next contraction stole her voice before she could tell him he'd have to start by unwrapping a scalpel. She prayed he wouldn't have to, because if he had to cut, he'd also have to stitch things up afterwards.

Was it her imagination, or were these contractions getting worse? Was this finally her transition stage? Not long now, if it was…

"Dilation is at ten centimetres."

Oh, thank the stars for the tablet's electronic voice.

"It's time. Help me up, Ghost," she said, using the gurney controls to get it into position to support her as she moved into a crouch on the bed. She gripped the railing on either side of her, resting her arms along it as she waited for the next contraction to hit.

"What should I do next?" Ghost asked.

"Get at the end of the bed. Be ready to catch when he comes out," she said. The baby would land on the bed, if she'd judged things right, but it was better to have him there, just in case. It also kept him from collapsing on them both if he fainted.

The urge to push hit her with the next contraction, and Maia knew not to resist it. She was ready. One push, then a breath, then another, and push…over and over, until…

"I think I can see the head," Ghost said, his calm voice cutting through the pain.

Maia's eyes flew open. "Really?"

His gaze held her tight. "Yes. You can do this, Maia. Keep pushing."

She couldn't look away from him now. With each push, she could feel herself growing weaker, heavier, like gravity was dragging her down…

"One more big push and it'll be out. Deep breath and…"

She let out a wordless shout as she put all her strength into this push. She could do this, they'd both survive this, and Kronos could suck vacuum.

"Stars, Maia, it's a boy!"

She felt a smile lift her lips, but it wasn't

over yet. "Hold him, and clamp the cord while I push out the placenta," she said.

So much easier than the birth. She let the bed down so that she could finally rest.

"Now give him to me, so you can put the cord in a stasis cannister, and dispose of the rest," she instructed. She lifted up her shirt so she could lay the newborn on her chest, while Ghost did everything she'd asked.

She shook her head, sure she'd witnessed a miracle – a man who could actually be an asset during a birth.

Ghost appeared at her shoulder. "Can I see him?"

Maia tugged down the neck of her shirt, so the baby's head appeared between her breasts. Baleful eyes regarded her for letting the cold air touch him.

"He looks like my grandfather. I can almost hear him say, 'Maia, have you been a naughty girl?'" Maia stared at the baby – her son. "I'll call him Christos, after my grandfather." She turned her beaming smile on Ghost. "Thank you. I'm not sure I could have done this on my own."

That's when she realised she'd lost her mind, because she kissed him.

TWELVE

Time stood still the moment Maia's lips touched his. Actually, the whole universe might have stopped – he wouldn't have noticed. She was all sweetness and light, passion and heat, the opposite to the cold vacuum of space, yet he was closer to going to pieces now than when she'd had him in the airlock. At the same time, it felt like every molecule in his body jostled together, closing the gaps between them, trying to get closer to

Maia. If he didn't stop it, his body was going to condense into something resembling a neutron star.

He forced himself to break the most incredible kiss he'd ever experienced, and the moment they parted, his knees wobbled, not wanting to hold him.

Grown men did not swoon, he told himself, as his spinning head threatened to make a liar out of him.

"I'll go see if I can find something to use as a cradle for the baby," he said. Even taking a single step away from her proved a massive effort. Perhaps she had a small singularity hidden in her pocket somewhere – something with a far more powerful pull than a mere neutron star.

Yet he managed it, one step after another, until he found himself in the galley. Not the sort of place he'd hope to find a cradle, but there was an empty box on the counter with the word MANGER printed on the side. A couple of blankets and it might do until he hunted up something better.

There was linen in one of the medbay cupboards, so he found blankets and sheets enough to turn the box into a passable cradle.

When he turned to offer it to Maia, though, he found she was fast asleep, with the baby cradled to her chest beneath her shirt. He didn't have the heart to wake them, so he left the box on the table beside her bed and headed off to find somewhere he could sleep, too.

THIRTEEN

The chime of an incoming call woke Maia. It wasn't the first time she'd woken since Christos was born – she'd had to put him in the makeshift cradle Ghost had left on the table – but this was the first time she wanted to leave her bed, instead of going back to sleep.

So she rose, donned a clean set of scrubs, then took Christos out of his cradle and put him on the gurney instead. Just as she'd suspected, the bed could reconfigure itself into something suitable for a newborn, now there was no adult patient on it. It could monitor his vitals, too, in case something went wrong. Not that anything should go wrong with such a healthy-looking child…

Maia shook her head. She'd scanned him countless times, and he showed no sign of adverse effects from Kronos's meddling with his DNA. Maybe he'd messed up and created a normal, healthy child instead of one of his superior beings.

For a moment, it seemed like a light shone on the boy's face and hair, before it faded.

Maia glanced around the medbay, looking for the light source, but she found nothing. Whatever it had been, it had gone out as quickly as it had appeared. Maybe just one of the gurney's scans, she told herself.

The chime sounded again, louder this time.

Maia padded out into the corridor, seeking the source of the chime.

It was coming from the cockpit, of course,

where Ghost lay draped across the pilot's seat, snoring.

The control panel wasn't locked any more, so she reached over and touched the glowing button that would answer the call.

"This is Colony Control. You're two hours late on your sitrep, Ghost," the woman on the screen said, not waiting for Maia's video feed to show she wasn't talking to Ghost. Well, not until he stopped snoring, anyway.

Maia pasted a professional smile on her face. "Greetings, Colony Control. My name is Maia and Mr Ghost here is resting."

The woman leaned forward and squinted at her screen. "Aren't you supposed to be in labour?"

Maia laughed. "With Mr Ghost's help, I delivered a healthy baby boy, weighing 3762 grams, at 0025 hours. Mother and baby are doing fine, thanks for asking."

The woman jerked back, as if to avoid a projectile. "I have a doctor on standby at the hospital, prepared to guide him through the labour, but..." She didn't seem to know what to do.

Maia had taken charge in far more difficult situations than this. "Tell him to stand down, as he won't be required for this one. However, Mr Ghost mentioned bringing me planetside so that your hospital can check me and Christos over. Perhaps I can meet your doctor in person, instead. Can you tell me when we'll have permission to land?"

"Our best estimate is three more days. The salvage crew found a larger number of stasis pods than expected, and..."

"From which ship?" Maia interrupted. Her last memory was of falling asleep in a stasis pod. If there were other survivors, perhaps they could tell her what had happened...

"The *Magellan,* an exploration vessel," the woman replied.

"The *Magellan* was a Human scout ship in the war. I was their medic," Maia said. "I can help – "

The woman nodded. "Stand by. I'll see if I

can clear the cargo bay any earlier. We need all the assistance we can get on this one. Fallon out."

The screen went dark.

"So, do you believe me now?"

Maia turned to find Ghost had woken up.

Somehow, during that hellish labour, she'd come to trust the alien, and she truly believed he didn't want to harm her. Any man who could hold his own during childbirth was more reliable than most. His stories about the Colony and peace, though…they seemed too good to be true.

"Show me your Colony, and I might believe you," she said.

Something flashed across the screen, making Ghost's eyes go wide.

"Fallon's found us a berth — the external cargo bay for Eden Dome. We can land when we're ready," he said, sounding like he didn't believe his own words. "Better buckle up, because we're going down."

Maia nodded. "I'll go secure Christos."

FOURTEEN

When the airlock doors opened, they were greeted by a grim-looking medevac team. That's how Fallon had gotten them landing clearance, Ghost realised.

"Where's the patient?" the doctor asked.

Maia stepped forward, one hand on the gurney that held her son. "Right here, Dr Shepherd."

The doctor blinked. "Maia? I thought you went down with the *Magellan*!"

Maia winked. "I took a nightshift nap in one of the pods they were using for hospital beds. Naps save lives, just like you told me."

"Not all of them. Some of the pods were so badly damaged, we can't even identify the occupants. Others needed extensive regen, and may never regain their memories. How come you're not with them?"

Maia grinned and linked arms with Dr Shepherd. "Tell me, did you ever hear stories about aliens kidnapping Earth girls for breeding experiments? It turns out some of the stories could be true."

The doctor, to her credit, didn't glance sideways at Ghost, though he half expected it. Maybe it was his Human coloured skin that placed him above suspicion. Heh. Maybe he'd keep this colour for a while longer.

Dr Shepherd's staff surrounded Christos's gurney and wheeled it off in Maia's wake.

Ghost wanted to go with them, but he stopped himself in time. His job was done – Maia didn't need him any more.

He turned his feet toward Control, where his clothes and a debrief with Fallon waited.

But he knew his heart went with Maia to hospital.

FIFTEEN

It wasn't until she was alone in a hospital room with Christos that Maia let the smile slip off her face. She'd been the professional space medic, nurse and midwife for far too long. Now, she was allowed to fall apart.

Sitting on the chair beside his bed, she cuddled the sleeping baby to her chest, and let the tears fall.

Kidnapped by an alien, forced to fight for her life, compelled to take command of the medbay while she laboured to give birth to a son she hadn't agreed to conceive or carry…and now, the biggest challenge of all: having to make her way as a new mother in a space colony all alone.

She wished she could bring Kronos back to life, like Ghost, so she could space him over and over and over again, maybe one piece at a time. She wasn't sure if it would truly make her feel better – hacking off limbs was hard! – but at least she'd be able to vent her frustrations on something.

What would really make her feel better would be another heart-stopping kiss from Ghost. Her cheeks grew hot at the thought.

He'd had to go off for debriefing, she knew, and his unit needed all hands on deck dealing with the survivors from the *Magellan* – which was where he likely would be next.

When they released her from hospital, she'd find out where his office was, and she'd go there to thank him.

But for now…she cried until the tears

stopped coming. Then it was Christos's turn, so she put him to her breast to quiet him. A little more colostrum couldn't hurt him.

That's how Dr Shepherd found her when she entered the room.

Maia looked up. "You going to tell me I'm breastfeeding wrong?"

It was a standing joke in maternity words across the galaxy that no two medical professionals could agree on the correct way to breastfeed a baby, but Dr Shepherd only smiled.

Ah. That meant she had serious things to discuss.

Maia finished up with Christos and put him back in his crib. Much more sanitary than an old lobster box.

"What is it?" Maia asked.

"As your doctor, I want to tell you that all Colonists are entitled to a full year of paid parental leave without any work responsibilities. You are well within your rights to refuse to do anything except what you feel is best for your child," Dr Shepherd began.

Maia knew there was a huge but coming.

"Under Senate salvage laws, as the only survivor about the *Burro*, a ship reported lost early in the war, you are sole owner of a licensed cargo hauler. You and your son could build a life as an interplanetary shipping contractor."

But Maia wasn't a pilot. She'd need a crew to do that, and flying wasn't what had brought her into space. Dr Shepherd knew that.

"The Colony Administration have authorised me to offer you a place here in the Colony, in this very hospital, in fact, as midwife, nurse or medic, depending on your preferences. They're willing to offer you a First Settler bonus of fifty thousand credits now, with a second such sum in five years, if you stay here that long. There's an additional bonus for having a mixed race child – a Titan-Human hybrid – but it only applies if you choose to stay here. Your assistance is requested as an independent consultant – at hourly rates higher than they pay me — to assist with the identification and rehabilitation of the *Magellan* survivors. Off the record, I can tell you it'll be a minimum of six weeks' work, and likely more — enough to pay for you to fly that space yacht around the system for a year, or, if you choose to stay here, you could trade it for one of the luxury family apartments anywhere in the Colony."

Dr Shepherd had supervised some of Maia's births back on Earth — and Maia knew the woman's professional opinion was worth listening to.

"What would you do?" Maia asked.

Dr Shepherd licked her lips as she looked at Christos. "If I had a son, I'd stay here. It's the only civilised planet in the system right now, and it could be decades before that changes. Take the consulting contract, to give you time to make a decision. Whether you'll stay or go, whether you want to work right away or wait, and where you'd like to live. Some of the luxury apartments in the Arbor Dome have gardens, the like of which you'd only find in the richest enclaves on Earth. Or the Ager Dome, where you get paid to grow fruit trees in your garden, and the fruit is yours, to do what you wish with." She hung her head. "But I admit I have an ulterior motive. We have only two qualified midwives in the entire Colony, and neither of the others can hold a candle to you. You trained a birth assistant while you were in labour. I don't know anyone else who could have accomplished such a thing. I need you, and I need you to help me train more, because people are starting to settle here, and once they do that, we'll be buried in babies. Every month will be September."

Maia laughed. "Stars forbid! One September a year is bad enough. But…what's the health care system like here in this Colony?"

Dr Shepherd spread her arms wide. "What you see here is standard. Universal healthcare across the Colony, available to all citizens, and better than public hospitals on Earth. Intelligent hoverbeds in every room, plus restricting staff hours to a normal work week. This is what healthcare was like for the Titans back in their system, and the peace treaty wouldn't allow for anything less. Oh, and childcare? It's free – the Colony Administration pay for it."

Life as a Colony midwife and mother. Maia knew that's what she'd choose, but it was best to take some time to see just what she was getting into before she said it aloud.

"I'll think about it," Maia said.

Dr Shepherd lowered her voice. "If it helps you make up your mind, I know a certain Emergency Services agent is single, and not for want of offers, either."

Trust a doctor to see more than anyone else. Maia managed a smile. "I'll think about it," she said again, though if she'd said him instead of it, she'd have been more honest, for Ghost was very much in her thoughts.

SIXTEEN

A message flashed up on Ghost's comm. His heart leaped at the thought that it was from Maia, but he came back down to earth when he saw it was from the housing office – his new house was finally finished, and he could move in today.

Perhaps that's what he needed – a few days off, moving house, settling in to the new place, to get his head straight. Stars knew he hadn't been thinking clearly since he met Maia. She hovered on the edge of his thoughts, no matter what he was doing. Every time he entered Metropolis City, he had to force himself not to walk into the hospital and ask to see her.

Like she'd want to see the alien she'd thrown out the airlock, and been forced to rely on to deliver her baby. Now she was in far better hands, she had no need for him.

It was for the best, he told himself.

So he collected his meagre belongings from his tiny box of an apartment – keeping costs low so he could save his money for a proper house – and headed out to the Arbor Dome.

A soft breeze rustled the leaves overhead, almost like real animals had been introduced to the forest, though he knew it was too early for that yet. Orel in Eden had told him birds would be first, and squirrels were at least a year away. If he played his cards right, he might be able to get one as a pet, or at least tame a wild one. Time would tell.

Past the ornamental lake and deeper into the trees he strode, all his possessions thrown into a bag he could carry over his shoulder. Then the trees started to thin, and he knew he was nearly home.

The first cabin he saw was exactly like he'd pictured it, likely because it was a life-sized version of the picture in the brochure. The synth-wood walls looked like real timber, rustic as some Earth re-enactment village on the outside, but as shiny and new as any apartment in Metropolis City on the inside. Each hidden from one another by trees, so it was almost like there was no one else in the world but you, in your log cabin and matching synth-wood fenced yard…

And there it was. Home.

Right on the edge of the compound, closest to the dome wall, a house bigger than he'd ever dreamed of having. All the overtime, all the danger pay, working every holiday, rescue mission after rescue mission during the war, risking life and limb over and over and over again…it had almost been enough. The loan to cover the rest wouldn't take him more than a few years to pay off, and his five-year First Settler bonus would cover the rest if he didn't pay it off by then.

Here he could find peace.

Ghost touched his hand to the reader at the entrance, and the door creaked open. He laughed aloud – the builders had done their work well. He pulled the door closed behind him, and breathed it in. Synth-wood walls and furniture added to the rustic charm, with windows – oh, how he'd missed windows – looking out on the forest in every direction.

Even the bed frames were made of synth-wood, in all four bedrooms. A pointless extravagance for a man who lived alone, but Ghost knew in his heart he didn't want to be alone forever. Maybe one day, when he no longer got flashbacks from the robot rebellion, or the war, or all those other disasters he'd like to forget, he'd hopefully find someone he wanted to share his life with.

He stared at the bed in the master bedroom, and his mind flashed to seeing Maia on that hospital gurney. Then the vision changed, so she reclined on the pillows on his bed instead.

He'd never seen anything he wanted so much. Maia, here, with him.

Her son would love the yard and the forest. Plenty of space for a boy to run. Christos could even have a room of his own, something few children in the Colony had in the basic family apartment configurations.

Madness, surely. For what would Maia want with an alien like him?

Then again, she was a single mother with nowhere to live. Maybe she'd appreciate a place to stay for a few weeks, until she found her feet.

Yes. He should pay her a visit, and make the offer, at least. If she refused, then he was no worse off than before. And if she accepted…stars, please let her agree.

SEVENTEEN

Ghost knocked on the open door to Maia's hospital room.

"More visitors? Who else could it be?" he heard Maia say. Then she raised her voice to call, "Come in!"

He rounded the corner and stopped dead at the sight of her. Pale blue scrubs replaced the green ones she'd worn on the *Burro,* with a name badge pinned to the front. She'd tied her hair back, too, and she was no longer barefoot.

If he'd passed her in the corridor, he might have mistaken her for one of the hospital staff.

Then her face lit with a smile. "Ghost!"

His breath caught in his throat as she hugged him.

Then she backed up, laughing shakily. "Sorry, I'm just so glad to see you. Gilda from the Records Office keeps asking about Christos's and my citizenship applications, Myra's been back and forth between Eden and the hospital, making sure everything's correct on her paperwork, and Frank from HR here at the hospital comes back every hour to offer me better terms, if I'd only sign the employment contracts for a job here. At least you haven't come bearing gifts of more paperwork!"

Ghost reluctantly lifted up the bag of his purchases from the hospital gift shop. "I got something for Christos. There wasn't much choice, but I thought maybe he'd appreciate a stuffed spaceship. It has a little bell inside, and this bit here, so you can hang it on the side of his crib..." He stopped babbling, and thrust the bag at her.

She peeked inside, smiled, then set it aside. "Thank you. I'll give it to Christos when the nurses bring him back from the nursery after his nap. In the meantime, I have a favour I want to ask you, though I know I have no right." She took a deep breath. "To register Christos's birth as a Colony citizen, there's a space on the form to list his father. Now, I can leave it blank, but if Kronos isn't dead and somehow comes back to claim him, I won't be able to stop him. Colony laws allow him to demand a DNA test, and if the child is his, I won't be able to stop him from claiming all the visitation rights a normal father might have. But if I were to put a name in that space, the name of a Colony citizen of good standing...Ghost, would you agree to let me put your name there? I'm not asking for anything else — no support, financial or otherwise — just your name on a piece of paper, to protect us both from that arsehole."

If his name alone could protect them from Kronos, Ghost would happily agree in a heartbeat. But he had to ask… "What will you tell Christos? When he asks who his father is?"

"I'll tell him that you're the man who stood beside me when he was born, and without you, neither of us would be here. That you're a hero who risked his life for ours, as I would for him. And while neither of his parents might share any DNA with him, given that he was conceived as one of that madman's experiments, he's still loved, because he's my son." Tears shimmered in her eyes, but she didn't shed them.

Ghost blew out a breath. He had to say this right, or she'd throw him out of a (metaphorical) airlock all over again. "I'd be honoured to be listed as Christos's father on his birth certificate, but I couldn't bring myself to just walk away with no responsibility. A father, even if just in name, doesn't do that to his son, or the mother of his son. I have…I have a house here in the Colony. Over in the

Arbor Dome. It's big enough for all of us, with a yard and everything, and you're welcome to stay as long as you want. I could even help take care of Christos, when you're working. As his father, at least on paper, I'd be entitled to paid parental leave, if you want me to…" He closed his eyes, hoping to delay the moment when she rejected him and everything he had to offer. She didn't need anyone else. She'd be absolutely fine without him, and she was going to say…

"You know, everyone's been telling me I should get an apartment in the Arbor Dome. With the sale of the *Burro* to Eden labs, I might be able to afford it, too. So thank you, I will take you up on your offer, at least for the next few weeks. After that, who knows? We might be neighbours."

He opened his eyes to find her staring wistfully at him. Neighbours, after being roommates. Better than a no – at least he'd still get to see her. And see if maybe, just maybe, he could convince her to stay. In the Colony, if not his house.

EIGHTEEN

Maia and Christos moved from the hospital the next day, to Ghost's beautiful house in the woods. Much like during the boy's birth, Ghost proved a fast learner, mastering nappies, bottle feeds and bathtime like he'd been born to be a father. Maybe he had.

She'd negotiated six weeks' leave after helping with the *Magellan* survivors, before she took up her position as midwife and clinical educator. They'd offered her the nurse manager's role — several times — but she'd turned it down. Let someone else manage the staff, she'd said. Her talents were better suited to the delivery room. They'd given her the title of Chief Midwife, swearing it came with no additional responsibility aside from being the most senior midwife on the ward, and she'd accepted.

One week ran into another, helped by Christos's erratic sleep cycles and arrival of the contents of the *Burro*'s kitchen, which Maia had not included in the ship's inventory when she sold it. So they had luxury rations to feed them for years, with a wine cellar to match. Not that either of them had touched the alcohol yet.

Every day she spent with Ghost, only made Maia's determination stronger. She didn't want to be his neighbour. No, she wanted to stay here forever. Let him be Christos's father in much more than name. And maybe, just maybe...

She didn't dare put her hopes into words, but held them tight in her heart all the same.

When the time was right, that would change. She just had to wait a little longer.

NINETEEN

Six weeks. Forty two days since Maia had come into his life, and they'd been the best days of his life. Ghost now knew he never wanted her to leave, but the deeper she slipped into motherhood and her job at the hospital, the less she needed him. She'd only been assisting with the other Magellan survivors so far, no more than an hour or two's work a day, but next week she'd start doing full shifts on the maternity ward.

She'd been at the hospital today, picking up her uniforms and taking care of last-minute paperwork, while Christos had spent his first day at the hospital creche. The creche staff had promised to contact him if he needed to pick up Christos early, but he'd heard nothing.

They didn't need him any more.

He'd be better off going back to work, where he'd be useful, instead of staying here in his empty house, wishing for what he couldn't have.

His heart lifted at the sound of Maia's voice, as it always did. A pity she didn't feel the same way, for she'd gone out of her way to avoid even the most casual physical contact while they shared a house together. Not that he'd tried to touch her, or said anything about his feelings for her. He hadn't dared.

Yet when she stepped into the living room, she threw her arms around his neck and kissed him. It was over before Ghost's brain had time to process this change, and then it just seemed to be filled with a sort of pink fizz.

Maia held up a sheaf of papers. "It's official! Christos and I are both Colony citizens…and First Settlers. Because he wasn't born in the Colony, I managed to argue that he was entitled to the same perks as any other child citizen, and the Registry Office agreed! Plus, the money from the sale of the Burro came through today. Which means we now have enough money to buy a home, and I know exactly which one I want."

Ghost's heart sank into his boots, but he fished out a smile and pasted it on his face. For Maia. "So, which place did you choose? One of the full size cabins, or one of the tiny houses they're just laying the foundations for? We'll still be neighbours, right?"

Her face fell, and he had his answer, before she'd even opened her mouth.

"Let me just put Christos to bed, and I'll tell you everything," she said. "He played all day in the creche, and fell asleep in the aircar. If the creche attendants are correct, we might be in for a full night's uninterrupted sleep. Now that's worth celebrating, eh?" She picked up his carrier and headed for his bedroom.

Ghost sighed. Though he didn't feel like celebrating, he couldn't bring himself to show anything but happiness for her success. She deserved it, after everything that had happened. A tiny voice in his head asked if he didn't deserve happiness, too, but he ignored it. Today was Maia's time to triumph.

When Maia finally returned, she'd changed into a nightgown he'd never seen before. Thin straps held the shimmery fabric in place over her shoulders, while the rest of it draped artfully over her curves to end at mid-thigh.

Ghost nearly dropped the bottle of champagne he'd liberated from the fridge, but caught it in time. "A celebration worthy of wine, or is it too early for that yet?"

Maia shrugged her shoulders. "I'm sure it's safe for me to have a glass or two. I have plenty of expressed milk on hand, so if Christos sleeps through the night, he should be fine with those until the alcohol's out of my system. If not…a couple of bottles of formula won't kill him. But…come sit with me. I'm sure the wine can wait a minute." She patted the couch beside her.

There was only one thing he wanted to do with her on that couch, and sitting wasn't it. Stars, he had to get his head straight. That nightdress was doing strange things to him.

His butt had barely touched the couch before she blurted out, "We're not going to be neighbours, Ghost."

He swallowed, then swallowed again. This wasn't about him – it was about what was best for Maia, and their son. "I understand. An apartment in Metropolis City would be closer to the hospital and the creche. Plus, all the restaurants – " He stopped as her finger touched his lips, hushing him.

"I've loved living here with you so much, Ghost, I don't want to leave, but I don't want to impose on you, either."

He opened his mouth to say she could never impose, that he loved having her here, loved her, but her hand still stopped him.

"So I made some enquiries about property prices, and this one in particular, and I discovered you have a mortgage on it. If you're willing, I'd like to pay for half the property, so we could be joint owners. I have enough to pay off the loan, and now everything here is settled, I can transfer the remaining credits for you to do what you like with." Her eyes looked troubled as she took her hand away. "What do you think? Is it a terrible idea?"

Ghost took a moment to remember how to speak. Words. Sentences. Stuff. "I think…it's a wonderful idea. One small change, though. Whatever credits you have left over, put them in a trust account for Christos." His heart felt so light, he feared it would float right out of his body. She was staying. She wanted to stay with him. "Can I open the champagne now?"

She fell back against the couch cushions. "Stars, yes! I was so scared you'd say no, and I'd never get to the second thing I wanted to ask you."

Whatever she asked for, he'd give it to her. He wanted to say the words, but he knew they'd sound crazy, so he busied himself with the champagne bottle instead. Vintage Earth wines were worth a fortune in the Altan system – if he spilled so much as a single drop and Nihal heard about it, she'd smack him into next week. Maia could live for a year off the money she'd make selling half the Burro's wine cellar to Vulcan, the manager of Forge, the club where Nihal worked. Maybe more. Or she could just keep it and drink it when she felt like it. Like tonight.

Ghost set out the glasses – real glass, because that's what good wine deserved – and poured with the kind of care that would make Nihal proud. Not that it mattered what his sister thought right now – Maia was the woman he wanted to impress tonight.

When he could delay no longer, he returned to his seat beside Maia and touched his glass to hers. "To the Colony's newest citizens, and First Settlers. We're honoured to have you both join us. The Colony will be a better place for new families, now and into the future, with you here."

Tears glistened in her eyes as she laughed weakly. "Hold on, hero. I've only delivered one baby in this system, and I needed your help for that. You're the one who spends all your time saving the Colony, not me, and definitely not Christos – not yet! I'd rather raise a toast to one of the Colony's heroes, a man who puts his life on the line for perfect strangers, even ungrateful ones who threaten to toss him out the airlock." Then she lifted the glass to her lips to drink.

Ghost took a sip, too. Stars, it was fizzy – there was a reason he preferred beer. Still, he managed to swallow before he set the glass down. "You didn't just threaten to toss me out the airlock. You actually did it, though no one outside this room knows it, and I'd prefer that it stays that way."

She nodded. They'd already discussed this – there was no mention of Kronos or the airlock in either of their reports. She didn't need to stand trial for murder or attempted murder, and Ghost didn't want to have to redo his training in hostile negotiations, which he'd be forced to do if Fallon knew how badly he'd failed in those first few minutes with Maia. So no one else knew she'd tried to kill him in self defence, or that he'd probably deserved it.

He definitely needed more wine. Ghost grabbed his glass and downed half of it.

"I have…a kind of confession to make, and an apology. Do you remember that time we kissed aboard the Burro?"

Ghost nodded. How could he forget? He'd dreamed about that kiss. And…other things, too.

"And have you noticed that, until today, I kind of tried to stay away from you, so I wouldn't do it again?"

Another nod. He wouldn't lie. Of course he'd noticed her keeping her distance, so she…wait, what?

She continued, "I've been avoiding intimacy

between us because I've come to realise I want more than just a kiss, and while my head might know what it wants, the rest of my body was still recovering from the birth. I mean, I've told so many new mothers they'd have to wait six weeks, but I never thought I'd have to remind myself…" Maia blushed. "Anyway, it's exactly six weeks today, and I insisted on them giving me a full medical at the hospital, just to make sure. So, if you'd like to start with a kiss, and see where that leads…" She looked up at him, her eyes filled with hope.

Anywhere and everywhere she wanted it to lead. "Yes, absolutely," Ghost said, reaching for her.

TWENTY

This time, Maia didn't pull away from Ghost's kiss. Six weeks of waiting…and now their time had come. He even liked the satin chemise she'd bought especially for the occasion. Though the way his hands were moving up her legs, he was soon about to discover that she hadn't bothered to buy underwear to go underneath it…

"Oh, Maia," he groaned.

She helped him out of his clothes, wanting

to see him naked again, like he'd been on the *Burro*. All hard muscle and dimples and…mmm. Yes, this was what she'd waited so long for, and who she'd waited to share it with. Stars, but his hands felt good. She wasn't going to get his pants off if he kept distracting her like that. Oooh…

"Do that again, and you can take your own pants off," she gasped out.

Ghost laughed, shucking off his pants like there was nothing to it. He reached for his underwear. "Are you sure, Maya?"

She pulled her chemise over her head. "Stars, yes, I've never been so certain of anything in my life."

Off came the underwear and ooh, was he ready for her. She just wanted to climb into his lap and…

Ghost swore softly. "I didn't think to get any contraceptives, and I don't have an implant, because they tend to disappear when I do my alien thing. So do any diseases, though, and I haven't even looked at another woman since I took form on the *Burro*."

She'd guessed as much.

He looked hopeful. "What about you? You have a contraceptive implant, right?"

She wet her lips. "It's not safe to have one until after I finish breastfeeding, and Kronos must have taken mine out before he put Christos in me. As for the diseases bit…I've never been with anyone before."

Ghost's breath whistled out through his teeth. "You're a virgin?" He made it sound like some sort of mythical creature.

She nodded once. "I never found a man I trusted enough to get naked with, and because I knew I wanted to join a space colony, I never really looked. Out here, with the war and all, I hadn't even thought about looking before…I found you."

"But…you've never…?"

"With a man, no. Or with a woman. I had some battery operated…toys…that I used in the privacy of my bunk on the *Magellan*. They're probably floating around in the asteroid belt somewhere, waiting to be found by some sex-starved salvage team..." Stars, she burst out laughing at that. Imagining some muscly asteroid miner picking up her bright blue vibrator and taking it back to his cabin...

She struggled to be serious. She had to ask him.

"And you want your first time to be with me?" Ghost looked shocked.

"Stars, yes." She pushed him down onto the couch and straddled his lap. He felt so hot between her thighs. Oh, how she wanted him, but she had to ask first.

"We should...we should wait until I can get some contraception. The last thing you want is another unplanned pregnancy so soon after the first. We should..."

Maia swallowed. "Only if you don't want to have a child with me. Christos could do with some brothers and sisters. You're already an amazing father. I can't imagine anyone more perfect to have a family with...or anyone I want to sleep with more. Unless you don't want..." She closed her eyes. If she'd guessed wrong...

"Maia, you don't know how much I do want. You, a family, all of it..."

Her eyes flew open. "Then sex, please, now, Mr Ghost." She tilted her hips, and he angled his, and ohhhh....yes.

They moved together, a perfect rhythm that accelerated faster and faster until it seemed the whole universe exploded into being around them, the birth of a million stars, fading until only two remained – the ones in his eyes as he stared at her.

"Stars, Maia, are you sure you've never done this before? That was...incredible..."

She beamed. "Yes, it was. You know what? I've heard the second time's meant to be even better than the first. Do you think we could...?"

"For you? Anything's possible. Once will never be enough."

"We should go to bed, then. Yours, not mine. Yours is bigger," she said. Then she had to wrap her legs around his waist as he picked her up and carried her to his bedroom.

A moment later, she was lost in his kisses, her hands on his body as his stroked her, until they collided once more, finding that rhythm that was both as old as the universe itself and as young as their love for one another.

"I love you, Ghost," she said, feeling it in her heart as surely as the knowledge that New Hope would keep spinning around the sun.

"Just like I love you, Maia, my Christmas miracle," Ghost panted.

She was close, so close, and she was certain he was, too.

And that's when it happened. Between one breath and the next, the universe stood still, for only a moment, but that moment was everything. And as Maia's vision returned, she decided aliens weren't so bad, after all. Especially ones with dimples.

Would you like to spend more time in the Colony? Read on for a sneak peek of the next book, *Vulcan*!

ONE

"Romance again? You can't be serious. Didn't we do that theme last month?" Sunita exclaimed.

Hestia shook her head. "Last month it was mysteries, then science, before this month's inspirational books. The month before that it was historical romance. Tomorrow we start romantic suspense. Totally different."

"They're both still romance subgenres," Reina chimed in. "Stars, there are enough of them to just run romance every month, and readers will borrow them. Everyone wants a little more love in their life, even if it's only the fictional kind."

"The fictional kind are always better than real life. They don't leave hair in the shower," Sunita said.

"So why are you complaining about having romance again?" Reina asked.

Sunita shrugged. "Because every time we have a romance theme, I have to deal with a bunch of cranky men readers who only want manly books, not girls' stuff."

"I can't believe misogyny still exists. Shouldn't we have bred it out of the Human race by now? Or the Titan one?" Reina complained.

"Misogyny isn't genetic, it's about environmental and emotional factors, particularly in childhood. Stamping out an idea isn't as simple as a genetic patch. Especially one as seductive as the thought that you're better than someone else, or a whole group of people," Hestia said.

"Like how people who read are more intelligent and interesting than people who don't?" Reina asked.

"Obviously," Sunita said.

Hestia couldn't argue with that. She was the Colony's only qualified librarian, after all. Reina and Sunita were both fast learners and extremely helpful in keeping the library running. Especially when New Hope was about to complete another orbit around its star, Altan, and they changed themes. A new year called for a new book, or at least that's what the sign over the themed display said.

It was more than just a new book for the three of them, though. On the last day of New Hope's year, they checked which books had been borrowed in the last month, put them onto the regular shelves, then took the unwanted ones downstairs for storage. At the same time, the printing presses got to work on the next set of themed books, printing brand new paperback copies from the electronic books in the archives, to fill those themed shelves for the next nineteen-day orbital period.

New Year's Eve was important. Out with the old, in with the new, and when they'd finished work for the day…

"Are you going there again tonight?" Sunita asked.

Hestia kept her eyes on the shelves she was stacking. "Going where?"

"You know."

Hestia sighed. "And what if I am?"

Sunita cocked her head to the side. "If I'd known, the first night I got invitations for the three of us and dragged you along, that you'd end up spending every New Year's Eve at Forge, drooling over the dancers like one of those misogynists at a peep show, I never would have taken you. It's not healthy, Hestia."

"That's not what you said before. That first time, you said it wasn't healthy for me to go home every night, and I needed to get out more. Now going out isn't healthy, either?" Hestia snapped. "And I don't drool. The dancers in Forge aren't strippers, either. They're performers, artists, and they do it with their clothes on. There's a reason tickets to Forge sell out every New Year's Eve. Everyone there wants to party, sending off the old year and ringing in the new, hoping for a fresh start."

"But not you," Reina said softly. "What's your new year's resolution this year?"

Hestia folded her arms across her chest. "The same as the last time I told you. To survive the year. I owe it to Ayumu."

The memory of the last time she'd seen Ayumu, raising their glasses together in a toast to a different new year, on a different planet, flashed through her mind for only a moment, but it was long enough to bring tears to her eyes. If only he were here. She had so much she wanted to say to him.

"You owe it to Ayumu's memory to live, not

just survive," Sunita scolded. "What you should do is make that your resolution tonight. To actually live. And then do it, if only for the next nineteen days. I guarantee you won't be drooling over dancers next New Year's Eve if you do."

She didn't drool. "I won't – " Hestia began hotly.

"Just try it," Reina coaxed. "It's less than three weeks. Most resolutions don't last that long, even with a normal Earth year. I'll tell you what. If you change your New Year's resolution tonight, we'll let you pick the next theme and we won't argue at all. You can have a whole year of poetry, even if you're the only one who'll read any of it."

"Not true. One of the library patrons keeps requesting a poetry theme every month. Seeing as we're doubling up on romance, to cater for the majority, it makes sense to give people what they should read, instead of just what they want every month. I bet we have a lot of people borrowing poetry books if we had that as a theme!"

Both women folded their arms.

"Make a new resolution, and we'll see," Sunita said.

Hestia knew when she was beaten. "We'll see," she echoed.

A new resolution wasn't so hard. It wasn't like she had to keep it. If they'd asked her to stay away from Forge, she wouldn't have agreed, but this…maybe. Maybe…

In the darkness of Forge, after the dancers left the stage, with a drink in her hand as they counted down the seconds, then she could make her decision. And not before.

TWO

Vulcan set the video to replay from the beginning. Something just wasn't right. Sure, it was a whirl of light and colour, the beat like a heart drumming the countdown to year's end, but he looked stiff, stilted, instead of the delicate flow of movement Wakana had always been able to demonstrate on this traditional New Year dance.

"Good news, boss. Nang Tani called and said the banana order should be here within the hour. Daquiris are back on the menu, thank the stars."

Vulcan didn't take his eyes off the video. "Thanks, Nihal. Can you take a look at this? It's missing something, and I can't work out what."

Nihal oozed around the desk — she was full-blooded djinn, so she could do that — and peered at the screen. After a long moment, she said, "Well, it's flat, boss, that's what it is. If you want people to fall asleep during the performance, it's fine, but if you want them to celebrate the New Year…you need fireworks."

Vulcan stared at the screen, then flicked his fingers. On the video, a light show erupted around the dancers, one that hadn't been there last time he watched the video. It still wasn't enough, though…

"You ever get tired of celebrating the New Year?" he asked. This would be his nineteenth New Year's Eve party in the Colony — one for every Academy dancer who'd died. He'd left Wakana 'til last because he knew he couldn't do her favourite dance justice. He looked…dead.

Nihal grinned. "Yep. About an hour or two after midnight, every time. When the show's over, right after I call for last drinks, everyone starts heading home, and I can see the end of my shift. Until then, I'll be the life of the party, keeping the drinks flowing, while you deliver another performance that'd make your Academy proud."

The Alba Academy of Dance was no more. He was the last one left. Yet energy and art never died, it stayed in the universe to inspire new forms in the future. At least, that's what Wakana had believed. And it was in her memory that he danced tonight. If she were here, she'd be rolling around on the floor, laughing her many tails off, at his piss-poor performance. He was a shambling zombie to her light-footed quest for perfection. Better to be a joker, a trickster, for Wakana said illusion and trickery lay at the heart of this dance.

Tonight would be the last performance, he

promised himself. A swan song, though he wouldn't be singing. He'd send Wakana out with the bang she deserved. If Nihal wanted fireworks, that's what she'd get. By the end of the night, nobody would be able to see, the celebration would blaze so bright.

And when the New Year began, it truly would be a fresh start.

ABOUT THE AUTHOR

Demelza Carlton has always loved the ocean, but on her first snorkelling trip she found she was afraid of fish.

She has since swum with sea lions, sharks and sea cucumbers and stood on spray drenched cliffs over a seething sea as a seven-metre cyclonic swell surged in, shattering a shipwreck below.

Demelza now lives in Perth, Western Australia, the shark attack capital of the world.

The *Ocean's Gift* series was her first foray into fiction, followed by her suspense thriller *Nightmares* trilogy. She swears the *Mel Goes to Hell* series ambushed her on a crowded train and wouldn't leave her alone.

Want to know more? You can follow Demelza on Facebook, Twitter, YouTube or her website, Demelza Carlton's Place at:

www.demelzacarlton.com

More Books by Demelza Carlton

<u>**Colony: Aqua series**</u>

Halcyon (#1)

Poseidon (#2)

Apollo (#3)

<u>**Siren of War series**</u>

Ocean's Justice (#1)

Ocean's Widow (#2)

Ocean's Bride (#3)

Ocean's Rise (#4)

Ocean's War (#5)

How To Catch Crabs

<u>**Nightmares Trilogy**</u>

Nightmares of Caitlin Lockyer (#1)

Necessary Evil of Nathan Miller (#2)

Afterlife of Alana Miller (#3)

Romance a Medieval Fairytale series

Enchant: Beauty and the Beast Retold

Dance: Cinderella Retold

Fly: Goose Girl Retold

Revel: Twelve Dancing Princesses
Retold

Silence: Little Mermaid Retold

Awaken: Sleeping Beauty Retold

Embellish: Brave Little Tailor Retold

Appease: Princess and the Pea Retold

Blow: Three Little Pigs Retold

Return: Hansel and Gretel Retold

Wish: Aladdin Retold

Melt: Snow Queen Retold

Spin: Rumpelstiltskin Retold

Kiss: Frog Prince Retold

Reflect: Snow White Retold

Roar: Goldilocks Retold

Cobble: Elves and the Shoemaker Retold

Float: Enchanted Horse Retold

Steal: Forty Thieves Retold

Call: Pied Piper Retold

Fall: Scheherazade Retold

Feather: Swan Maidens Retold

Cross: Billy Goats Gruff Retold

Weave: Rapunzel Retold

Claim: Puss in Boots Retold

Curse: Rose Red Retold